THE FABLES of AESOP

THE FABLES
of
AESOP

RETOLD BY
FRANCES BARNES-MURPHY

COLLECTED AND ILLUSTRATED BY
ROWAN BARNES-MURPHY

Lothrop, Lee & Shepard Books   New York

First Edition 1 2 3 4 5 6 7 8 9 10

Library of Congress Cataloging in Publication Data

Barnes-Murphy, Frances. Aesop's fables/as retold by Frances Barnes-Murphy ; illustrated by Rowan
Barnes-Murphy.
p.   cm. Summary: A collection of fables retold from Aesop, including "The Hare and the
Tortoise," "The Ant and the Grasshopper," and "Androcles and the Lion."   ISBN 0-688-07051-5 (RTE)
1. Aesop's fables—Adaptations. [1. Fables.]   I. Aesop.   II. Barnes-Murphy, Rowan, ill.
III. Title. PZ8.2.B196As 1994 398.22'5—dc20   [E] 93-48462 CIP AC

The illustrations in this book were done in ink and watercolor on Fabriano watercolor paper.
The display type was hand-lettered by Rowan Barnes-Murphy. The text type was set in Palatino.
Printed and bound by New Interlitho. Production supervision by Esilda Martinez.
Designed by Rowan Barnes-Murphy.

To Evelyne Johnson, Dorothy Briley, and Susan Pearson

with thanks

RBM

To the memory of my grandmother, B. West

FBM

THE FABLES of AESOP

COLLECTOR'S NOTE

I've particularly enjoyed compiling and illustrating this collection of *Aesop's Fables*. Not only has the project given me the chance to get reacquainted with dozens of half-forgotten favorites, but I also discovered many delightful tales that were entirely new to me.

Some of the fables compiled here, such as "The Tortoise and the Hare" and "The Fox and the Grapes," are included simply because no collection of Aesop's fables would be complete without them. Others are included because I particularly enjoyed them, or because they conjured up images I thought would be interesting to illustrate. But I've tried to represent the scope of the entire Aesop canon while cutting it down to a manageable size. During my research, I found a vast number of fables from many lands and cultures, all attributed to Aesop—over five hundred of them!

In some collections each fable is capped with a moral epigram. But these morals are thought to be later additions to the fables, probably dating from medieval times. Many of them, such as "Don't count your chickens before they're hatched," "Slow but steady wins the race," and "Honesty is the best policy," have been so over-quoted that they have become cliches. I have elected to tell the stories as Aesop would have, leaving readers to discover for themselves the universal truths they contain.

Very little is known about Aesop. Over the twenty-five centuries since he lived, the few historical facts about the man have become hopelessly entangled with the myth. He was described as ugly, and he may have had a speech impediment and other handicaps. Aesop may also have been of Ethiopian extraction, but this is all conjecture.

We know that around 600 B.C. a man called Aesop was born into slavery, probably on the Greek island of Samos. Telling fables would have been a valuable talent for a slave. Amusing tales with deeper meanings let slaves voice their opinions or even criticize their masters without fear of reprisal. Aesop's clever fables brought local fame and fortune to him and his master, Iadmon, who eventually freed him.

Word of Aesop's genius spread, and he was summoned to the court of Croesus, king of Lydia, one of the most powerful rulers of his time. Croesus was so impressed with Aesop that he commissioned him as an ambassador and sent him on important diplomatic missions.

Aesop died while on a mission from Croesus to the people of Delphi. Some records say that a sacred cup from the Delphian temple of Apollo was found in Aesop's luggage. Others say that a dispute arose over a payment Aesop was delivering, and he sent it back to Croesus. Whatever the reason, the enraged Delphians executed Aesop.

Aesop never wrote down his stories, but they lived on, passed from mouth to mouth. About two hundred years after his death, an Athenian scholar, Demetrius Phalereus, finally wrote down about two hundred fables in his *Aesopia*. No complete copy of Demetrius's manuscript survives, but early in the first century of the Christian Era, a Greek freedman, Phaedrus, translated Demetrius's *Aesopia* into Latin verse (adding a few fables of his own to it). Later in the same century, a Roman poet, Valerius Babrius, published Aesop's tales in Greek, along with fables from the Middle East, Africa, and India. These collections, and that of an anonymous Latin writer that survives as *The Augustina*, are the sources of what we know today as Aesop's fables.

THE TORTOISE AND THE HARE

One day a hare was in the mood for a good fast race, but could only find a slow old tortoise to challenge. "It's no good asking you to race," the hare complained rudely, "because you are the slowest creature I know. It's a wonder you ever get anywhere."

The tortoise smiled and said, "How can you be so sure? Remember the barn at the far end of the farm? I will race you there!" And with that, the old fellow plodded off, leaving the astonished hare behind.

"What a joke!" the hare said to himself. With a leap and a bound he overtook the tortoise and disappeared into the distance. He ran at top speed for a mile or two but was finding this race no fun at all. He sat down and said, "I'll wait here, and when he catches up, I'll zoom by at the last minute and win!" The hare waited and waited. He dozed off to sleep in the heat of the sun, and soon he was snoring. As the sun went down late in the afternoon, the tortoise plodded by. The hare slept on peacefully. When he awoke, he jumped up and dashed to the finish line. Much to his surprise and dismay, the tortoise was already there!

THE FOX AND THE GRAPES

A fox was out for a walk one evening. When he came to a vineyard where the grapes were ripe and plentiful, he realized he was hungry. The fox licked his lips at the sight of the lush fruit that hung temptingly above his head. He stood up on his hind legs to pull a bunch from the vine, but he couldn't reach it. He tried again, stretching as tall as he could, but the grapes remained beyond his grasp. Finally he leaped up and snapped at the fruit with his powerful jaws, but to no avail. At last the fox turned and sauntered out of the vineyard. With a flick of his tail, he said, "Let someone else have them. Those grapes are sour."

THE EAGLE AND THE JACKDAW

 jackdaw watched with much admiration as an eagle swooped out of the sky, seized a lamb with its talons, and carried it away Inspired to do the same, the jackdaw pounced on a lamb, but his claws became caught in its fleece, and he could not free himself. A shepherd came to the lamb's rescue and set both the jackdaw and the lamb free. The shepherd's children asked him, "What kind of bird is that?" He replied, "He is a jackdaw who thinks he is an eagle."

THE OLD WOMAN AND THE WINE CASK

 n old woman came across a wine cask and tipped it up to her mouth, but it was empty. However, the fragrance of the wine was infused into the wood, causing her to exclaim, "What a superior wine this must have been, to leave behind such a delicious aroma!"

THE FROGS AND THE BULLS

cross a meadow, a frog saw two bulls fighting for the right to lead the herd. "Oh dear, whatever will become of us?" cried the frog nervously. The other frogs did not understand his fears, for how could a quarrel between two bulls involve them? The frog explained, "The winning bull will stay with the herd, but the losing bull will make his escape through these marshes and trample us to death."

THE FROG AND THE OX

group of young frogs playing in a meadow were surprised by an ox, who began to graze nearby. Alarmed by his size, they rushed home to tell their mother. She puffed herself out grandly and asked, "Who is the larger, the ox or me?"

Much to her displeasure, her children said, "The ox!"

Angrily she swelled herself more and asked, "Now who is the larger?"

Again the answer was, "The ox!"

On hearing this, she made a huge effort. She puffed and swelled to an enormous size, and then she exploded!

DOCTOR FROG AND THE FOX

A frog emerged from the water, sat upon a lily pad, and announced boldly, "I am a gifted physician! Come to me if you are sick, for I can cure all ills, and no one will be turned away!" The animals who heard this proclamation murmured their admiration and gratitude. A fox, however, was not so impressed, and said to the frog, "If you are such a talented doctor of medicine, why haven't you cured your own croaky voice and warty skin before you presume to heal others?"

THE TWO FROGS AND THE WELL

During a long hot summer, the pond where two frogs lived dried up. When the rain failed to come, the frogs left their home in search of water. Sometime later they passed a deep well and stopped to look down. On seeing the water below, one frog said to the other, "Why not make this our new home? Look at all the water down there!"

The second frog was more cautious and replied, "There may be water down there now, but if it dries up, how will we ever get out again?"

THE YOUNG MOUSE

 young and innocent mouse came home from his first adventure and told his mother what he had seen. "I met a tall, loud, brightly colored fellow, red and yellow and brown, with a sharp, hard nose. Then there was a beautiful golden creature, with fur and ears much the same as yours and mine, and a long smooth tail. He was most likely related to us! He smiled kindly at me and wanted my company, but that noisy fellow came along again, and screeched and flapped until I was so frightened that I ran home."

His mother said, "The one you describe as friendly was our most deadly enemy, the cat, and the other was the rooster, who certainly saved your life. Learn from this, that appearances can be deceptive."

THE MOUSE AND THE WEASEL

 weasel was watching a small, thin mouse as it slipped through a hole in the side of a grain basket. Once inside, the hungry mouse gorged herself on corn until she was swollen with food and could eat no more. But when the mouse tried to leave the basket, she could not fit through the same hole, and was trapped. The weasel approached the basket and called to the mouse, "My friend, you were half-starved and lean when you went in through that hole, and you will be the same way before you come out!"

THE TOWN MOUSE
AND THE COUNTRY MOUSE

 mouse lived in the country, under a holly hedge. Expecting a visit from her old friend who lived in town, she made her simple home as clean and comfortable as possible. It was winter and food was scarce, so she scoured the fields and hedgerows for scraps for her guest to eat. The country mouse was pleased to see her friend, who looked plump and prosperous. The town mouse, however, was secretly shocked to see her friend so thin and poor. The room was bare and damp, and the meal so meager that after they had finished, she was still hungry. "You should not live this way," she said firmly. "Come to town with me, and see how well I do."

The country mouse was thrilled to see her friend's beautiful home. It was very grand, with every comfort. On the dining-hall table were the remains of a magnificent banquet. As they feasted, they were disturbed by noisy servants. The mice hid until it was safe and then made their way to the pantry, but they had to be careful, for there were dogs in the house. In the kitchen, they were nearly caught by the cook's cat!

The country mouse said, "This is no home for me. I am returning to the country, where I will be poor but safe and have peace of mind."

THE TWO BAGS

Every man has two bags around his neck, one slung over his chest and the other over his back. Each bag is full of human faults. The bag in front of the man, in full view, contains the faults of others, while the bag on his back, which is difficult for him to see, contains his own.

THE FOX AND THE TURKEYS

A fox came upon a tall tree and, looking up, he saw some turkeys in the branches. He was determined to have them for his supper. The tree was a good lookout and fortress, and the turkeys could easily see the fox by the light of the moon. The fox started to dance as the turkeys watched. Round and round the tree he tripped and swirled and gamboled. Never daring to take their eyes off him, the turkeys began to sway. On he went, first a jig, a rumba, and a waltz, then the can-can, the samba, and of course the foxtrot, his favorite. All the while, the turkeys watched, and the fox danced faster and faster, until the dizzy birds began to wobble. He danced on relentlessly, until, one by one, the turkeys fell out of the tree, just as the fox had intended.

THE COCK'S ALLY

A cock and a dog became fast friends and fell into the habit of traveling together. At night the cock would go to the top of a tree to sleep, and the dog would curl up in a hollow at the bottom. Each morning the bird awoke and crowed from the top of the tree to tell the world that it was time to get up.

One morning, a hungry vixen was awakened by the crowing and made her way to the base of the tree. She called up to the cock, "What a fine voice! Please come down, for I would like to thank you personally for waking me in such a pleasant way this morning."

The cock said, "I will come down as soon as I can. Meanwhile, why don't you rest in the hollow of the tree?" The vixen agreed and entered the hollow. There she met the dog, who growled viciously and chased her deep into the forest.

24

THE DOG AND HIS REFLECTION

A dog was walking by a stream, carrying a bone, when he noticed his reflection in the water. Thinking the image was another dog, carrying a larger bone, he dropped his own and attempted to snatch the larger one. The real bone was swept downstream, and so the greedy dog went home with none.

1 Tim. 6:8

THE OLD HOUND

An old hound was out hunting with his master when he came across a wild boar and seized it by the ear. The wild boar squealed and kicked and struggled, until the old hound tired and couldn't hold on anymore. The wild boar escaped.

The master was full of rage, and he shouted and swore at the old dog. The hound replied, "I still have the will to be a hunter: it is just my old muscles that let me down. Instead of chastising me for my weakness, you should praise me for what I once was."

Heb 3:13a

THE MONKEY AND THE DOLPHIN

During a violent storm at sea, a ship went down just off the Greek mainland and all hands were lost. There was one survivor. A small monkey clung to a piece of wreckage and he, too, would have perished before long, but for a dolphin who came to his rescue. The dolphin had not seen a monkey before and assumed him to be a human.

Full of concern for the survivor, the dolphin said, "Climb onto my back and I will take you ashore. Do you know anyone in Athens?"

The monkey, who was very pleased to be thought human, replied, "Yes, indeed, I am from one of the very best Athenian families!"

The dolphin said, "Then you must know Piraeus."

The monkey answered cheekily, "Of course! Everyone knows Piraeus. He is a good friend of the family."

The dolphin was enraged, for Piraeus is the port of Athens, not a man's name, and so he knew the monkey to be a liar. Without hesitation, the dolphin dived to the bottom of the sea, leaving the monkey to fend for himself in the waves.

Pro 3:7
Rom 12:3,16

THE WOLF AND HIS SHADOW

s the sun went down, a wolf noticed how large and menacing his shadow was and wondered why he had ever been afraid of the lion. "I must be a giant of a wolf to throw such a shadow," he said. "I could be king of all the animals!" But as he spoke, a huge, awesome shadow sat down next to his. He turned to see the lion, who struck the wolf down with one mighty blow.

(Pr16:18)
Don't measure
your shadow
at sunset.

THE WOLF AND THE LAMB

wolf was drinking at a brook one day, when he noticed a young lamb, lapping at the water. Although the wolf had just eaten and was not hungry, he decided to kill the lamb anyway, but felt he must have some sort of excuse. In a loud voice he accused the lamb of muddying the drinking water. "That is not possible," said the lamb politely. "I am downstream of you."

Pro 19:3?

The wolf thought again. "It was you who insulted my father last year!" he growled.

"But I wasn't born until this year," protested the lamb.

"Then it was your brother!" insisted the wolf.

"I have no brother," was the reply.

In exasperation the wolf said, "I do not care for your excuses, so I will eat you up!"

THE WOLF AND THE LION

A wolf had seized a sheep and was going home when a lion snatched his prize away. The wolf cried out angrily, "How dare you take what is rightfully mine!"

The lion laughed and said, "Why should I believe this sheep is yours, when all the world thinks you stole it?"

No one believes a liar, even if he's right.

THE WOLF WHO TURNED FLUTE PLAYER

A goat was about to be killed by a wolf. In the hope of saving his skin, the goat asked to hear the sound of a flute for the last time. The wolf, seeing no reason to refuse this one reasonable request, played the goat's favorite melody. The strains of the music were heard by nearby dogs, who came to see what was happening and chased the wolf away. He ran off saying, "I was a fool to play at being a musician when I had work to do."

THE ASS AND HIS SHADOW

A man who was journeying to a distant town hired an ass, with a driver, for the trip. As the day wore on, the sun beat down upon the man until he became uncomfortably hot. He decided to rest in the shadow of the ass. But the driver took issue with him, arguing that the man had hired only the ass and not the shadow, and therefore only the driver was entitled to sit in the shade. They became more and more irate with each other and finally came to blows. Meanwhile, amid the uproar, the ass trotted off, unnoticed.

THE SICK LION

An old lion became so weak and ill he was no longer able to hunt for food. He retreated to his den, where other animals came to call on him. As soon as a visitor came within his reach, the lion would take the opportunity to have a hearty meal. One evening the fox arrived and, keeping a safe distance from the lion, asked how he was feeling. The lion whispered, "Come closer, my friend, and comfort me in my last hours."

The fox wasn't fooled. He answered, "Excuse me if I do not, for I have observed that tracks lead toward your den, yet none point the other way."

THE MILLER, HIS SON, AND THE ASS

A miller and his son set off to market to sell their ass. Wanting the animal to reach the sale in good condition, they walked at its side. They met a group of young girls who mocked them, saying, "What simpletons, walking when they could ride!"

Feeling foolish, the miller told his son to ride the rest of the way. Later, a group of gentlemen passed by and said in disgust, "Thoughtless young man! Look at him riding, while his poor father walks."

The miller's son pulled his father up onto the ass, and they continued their journey. Passing a group of women, they heard the comment, "What a cruel way to treat an animal, overloading it so."

Shamefaced, the man and boy dismounted, tied the ass by its legs onto two poles, and carried it to town. As they approached the market square, people turned to stare and laughed when they saw the trussed-up ass.

The noise and discomfort became too much for the poor animal, which broke free and disappeared into the crowd. The miller and his son went home dejected. They could please nobody and had lost their ass in the bargain.

THE WILD BOAR AND HIS TUSKS

A fox was amused to see a wild boar making a great display of sharpening his tusks on a tree stump. "Why are you sharpening your tusks?" he asked.

The wild boar replied, "In case of danger."

The fox ostentatiously looked all around, then sneered, "I can see no danger."

The wild boar continued to work, saying, "Danger can come at any time and I shall be ready for it."

THE TWO TRAVELERS AND THE AXE

wo travelers came upon an axe in the road. One picked it up and said, "Look what I have found!" Later in the day, a huge man came in pursuit of them, angrily claiming that his axe had been stolen. "We are in a spot of trouble now!" said the man with the axe nervously.

His companion replied, "I'm sure you intended to say I, not we! You cannot expect me to share the danger, when you were unwilling to share the axe."

THE LEOPARD AND HIS SPOTS

leopard was very proud of his beautiful coat, particularly of its fine markings. Comparing himself with the other animals, he thought that their coats fell far short of his, and this made him feel very superior. His highhanded ways were resented by the other animals, and the fox felt it was time to put the leopard in his place. He said, "Having a few spots on your coat does not make you better than the rest of us. What is important is what you have inside you, not how you look from the outside."

THE HARE AND THE HOUND

A hound was giving chase to a hare, but she outran him, and he lost her. When he stopped to catch his breath, an on-looker sneered, "That old doe was faster than you!"

The hound replied, "Yes, she was, for she was running for her very life, while it was merely a dinner that I was after."

THE DOG'S BELL

A young dog enjoyed snapping at people's heels when they least expected it. His master could not cure his bad behavior, so he attached a large bell to the dog's collar as a warning to one and all. The dog was immensely proud of this bell and swung his head from side to side as he walked, to make sure it rang loud and clear.

An old hound asked him, "Why do you deliberately ring that bell?"

The dog replied, "Because I am so proud of it!"

The old hound said, "You should understand that the bell is not a prize to be treasured, but a disgrace. It labels you as a menace to be avoided."

THE OAK AND THE REED

An oak standing proud and still by a riverbank was ashamed of a nearby reed, which bent and swayed in the wind. "Why do you allow yourself to be pushed around in that way?" the oak asked crossly. "Stand tall and strong, as I do." One day there was a terrible storm and the wind whipped and lashed until the oak could take no more and fell with a mighty crash. The reed continued to bend backward and forward, and when the storm subsided, was no worse for wear.

THE HUNTER AND THE WOODSMAN

A hunter met a woodsman and asked if he had seen any lion tracks. "Yes indeed!" said the woodsman helpfully. "I know exactly where a lion is at the moment, and I will be pleased to take you there right now."

The hunter blanched and stammered his thanks to the woodsman, adding, "I really only wanted to see the tracks, not the lion."

THE BOY WHO CRIED "WOLF!"

A young shepherd boy was fond of playing jokes on others. While tending his sheep, he had plenty of time to think of pranks. One day he shouted at the top of his voice, "Wolf! Wolf!" The villagers came running to his assistance, only to find the sheep grazing peacefully and no wolf in sight. The boy enjoyed his joke so much that he teased the villagers with it again and again. One day a hungry wolf really did appear and began chasing his sheep. The desperate shepherd cried, "Wolf! Wolf!" to summon help, but the villagers just sighed and said, "It's only that silly boy playing jokes again," and went about their business. The shepherd shouted and shouted, but the villagers took no notice and the unfortunate boy lost his flock.

THE DOG IN THE MANGER

A dog took to sleeping in a manger. When the horses came there to eat, the dog growled at them to go away. One horse said to another, "He won't let us eat, yet he can't eat the oats himself."

THE MAN AND THE SATYR

A man traveling through a forest was joined by a satyr, and as they walked they fell into friendly conversation. The weather was cold, and feeling the chill, the man blew upon his hands. "Why do you do that?" the satyr asked curiously. Amused by his companion's innocence, the man explained that it was to warm them. They stopped to rest for the night, and the man built a fire and made broth. He took up his bowl, but the broth was piping hot, and so he blew upon it. "Why do you blow now?" asked the surprised satyr.

"To cool the broth," the man replied.

With that the satyr jumped up and ran off, saying, "I cannot stay with a man who blows hot and cold with the same breath!"

THE GOAT, THE KID, AND THE WOLF

A mother goat had to leave her kid at home alone, so she gave him strict instructions not to open the stable door to strangers. A hungry wolf overheard this conversation. As soon as she was out of sight, he knocked on the door and pretended to be the mother goat returning for something she had forgotten. Although the voice sounded just like his mother's, the kid looked out of the window before opening the door. He called to the wolf, "Go away! You sound like my mother, but you look too much like a wolf to be trusted."

THE WOMAN AND THE HEN

A woman kept a hen and tended the bird well. For her efforts she was rewarded each morning with a nice fresh egg, which she ate for her breakfast. She decided she needed more eggs than this, but rather than buy another hen, the woman fed her bird twice as much corn, expecting twice the number of eggs. From that day forward, however, the hen grew big and fat and lazy and stopped laying altogether.

THE COCKS AND THE HENS

Two cocks were fighting over the hens and, when the battle was over, the winner flew to a rooftop and crowed for all he was worth. The loser hung his head in shame and dragged himself into a dark corner of the farmyard to be alone. Before the winner could enjoy his victory, an eagle swooped out of the sky, seized him, and carried him away. The other cock, seeing his rival gone, came out into the open and took his place with the hens.

HERCULES AND THE CARTER

carter was driving along a rutted lane and carelessly allowed his wagon to become stuck in a muddy ditch. The foolish man gazed helplessly at the mess without lifting a finger and prayed to Hercules for aid. The god answered him by saying, "You cannot expect help from others if you do not first help yourself."

THE TWO FRIENDS AND THE BEAR

Two friends, who were traveling companions, promised to help each other through thick and thin. One day they were surprised by a bear. One man escaped by climbing a tree, but the other was too slow. Completely at the bear's mercy, he fell upon the ground and played dead, sure that his friend would come to the rescue. The bear approached the fallen man and sniffed around his mouth and ears. The man held his breath, and the bear assumed him to be dead and walked away. Greatly relieved, the other man jumped down from the tree and helped his friend up, asking, "What did the bear whisper in your ear?"

The man answered, "He said that I should take care to choose my traveling companions more wisely, for a true friend would not desert me in time of trouble."

THE HUNTER AND THE LION'S PICTURE

An old man dreamed that his only son, a natural sportsman and hunter, was killed by a lion. Being terribly afraid that the dream might come true, the worried father built a large barn and locked his son away in it. To make it less like a prison, he decorated the walls with pictures of animals and faraway places. Even so, the son begged to be set free, but his father was afraid to let him out. The young man felt particularly angry and frustrated when he looked at the picture of a lion. One day he stood before it and shouted, "It's your fault I am pent up in here!" With that he smashed the wall with his fist, and a small splinter of wood became embedded in his hand. The next day his hand was inflamed, and quickly the infection spread throughout his body until he became weak and died. His father was wracked with grief and cried, "I tried to change his fate, but a lion killed him anyway."

THE BULL AND THE GNAT

A gnat alighted on a bull's horns and rested there a few moments. When it was time to move on he told the bull, "I will be going now," and added politely, "I hope I didn't inconvenience you too much."

The bull answered, "Not at all! And, as I never felt your presence, it makes no difference to me if you go or stay."

THE CROW AND THE FOX

A fox was walking by a tall tree and looked up to see a crow perched high in the branches. The fox noted with considerable interest the large cheese the crow held in her beak. He called out, "What a pity that a bird such as you, with the finest of feathers, the brightest of eyes, and the most graceful of necks, cannot sing. Without doubt, your song would be the loveliest song of all."

On hearing these words, the crow preened herself with pleasure, then opened her beak and croaked for all she was worth. The prized cheese fell to the ground, and the fox ate it up with great relish. As he departed, the fox said, "You have a loud voice, crow, but you have no brains."

THE SWALLOW AND THE YOUNG MAN

A foolish young man had spent his inheritance, so he had to sell everything he owned to pay his debts. All he had left were the clothes he stood up in, which included a good warm overcoat. On a spring morning he spotted a swallow and had the happy thought that summer had arrived. With that, he hurried off to sell his overcoat and spent the rest of the day frittering the money away. The next day, however, the fickle spring weather had changed, and it was frosty and cold. Miserable and shivering, the young man found the swallow lying dead upon the ground and said, "Unhappy bird! Your early arrival has ruined us both."

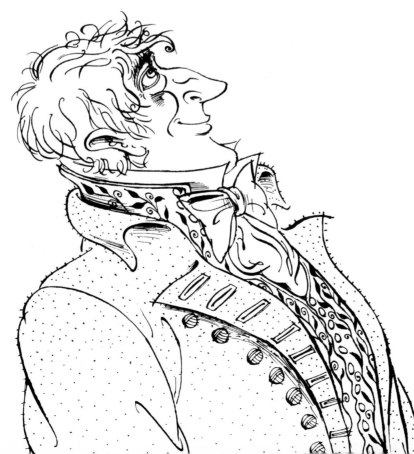

THE MARRIAGE OF THE SUN

It was rumored that the sun was about to be married, and the frogs were excited at the idea of festivities that would mark the occasion. They were brought back to earth, however, by a dreary old toad, who said, "Why all the merriment? One sun alone dries up our muddy pools in summer. What will become of us if the sun's marriage produces many little suns?"

THE NORTH WIND AND THE SUN

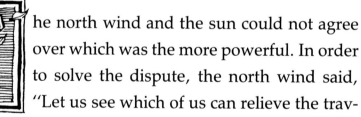

The north wind and the sun could not agree over which was the more powerful. In order to solve the dispute, the north wind said, "Let us see which of us can relieve the traveler of his cloak." With this the wind blew up a gale. The cloak billowed out, but the man became cold and wrapped it tightly around himself. No matter how the north wind lashed and tugged at the cloak, the traveler held on and would not let go. Then it was the sun's turn to try. It blazed in the sky until the man was soon overcome by the heat and removed the cloak.

THE FATHER AND HIS SONS

A father was distressed because his sons were always fighting and quarreling. One day he gave each of them a bundle of sticks and told them to break the bundles in two. The boys struggled hard but could not do so. The father showed them that when they separated the bundles and broke the sticks one at a time, the task was easy. He explained, "The same applies to you, my sons. Together you are strong, but separately you are vulnerable to your enemies."

HERMES AND THE SCULPTOR

The god Hermes wondered how mere mortals felt about him, so he disguised himself as a traveler and visited a sculptor's workshop. He admired the man's work and asked the price of several pieces. Then, pointing to a statue of himself, he said, "This statue of Hermes must be your most valuable work. How much do you charge for his likeness?" The sculptor answered, "I will make a deal with you. If you pay me what I ask for both Hera and Zeus, you can have Hermes for free."

HERMES AND THE WOODSMAN

 woodsman was high up in a tree, chopping off dead branches, when he dropped his axe into the lake below. He was deeply distressed for he could not afford another. Hermes took pity on the woodsman. The god dived deep into the lake, emerged from the water with a golden axe, and offered it to the woodsman, who said, "I cannot take this, for it is not mine." Hermes dived again and brought a silver axe to the surface. The man refused this valuable axe as well, so Hermes went down again and found the woodsman's missing axe. To reward him for his honesty, Hermes gave the woodsman all three axes. On returning home, the woodsman told his friends the story of his good fortune. One cunning fellow thought he might try his luck. He dropped his axe into the lake, then pretended to be in despair. Hermes came to his aid and offered him, too, a golden axe. The man accepted the axe as his own. This so angered Hermes that he threw the golden axe back into the lake and left the deceitful man to go home empty-handed.

THE FARMER AND THE STORK

A farmer placed nets in his fields to catch those who had been stealing his corn, and among the usual crows and geese, he caught a single stork. The stork pleaded with the farmer to spare his life, saying, "I am no crow or goose, but a stork. I will never do it again. Please do not harm me!" The stork went on in this vein until the farmer's patience ran out. He said, "You deserve the same fate as the others, whatever you say, for you were in their company."

THE STORK WHO DINED WITH A FOX

A fox who enjoyed practical jokes had thought up a good trick to play on a stork. He invited her to dinner and served her thin soup in a shallow dish, knowing full well that her long beak would make it impossible for her to eat a drop. He enjoyed his joke very much and let her go home hungry. The following week, the stork returned the fox's invitation. Dinner was served and it smelled delicious but, much to his dismay, the food was in a tall jar with a neck so narrow it was quite impossible for the fox to reach even a morsel. The hostess made a great show of enjoying her meal, while the fox had to make do with lapping up the little drops she spilled. He went home still hungry and told himself, "I set the example, so I can't complain at being paid back."

THE DONKEY AND THE LAPDOG

The master of the house was very fond of his lapdog. The dog was lovable and friendly, always jumping up and barking, and full of fun. Whatever the little dog did, the master laughed and petted him, and sometimes gave him special tidbits.

A hardworking donkey saw all this and was determined to share the master's favor. One morning he broke free from his harness and rushed into the house to greet the master as he awakened. The donkey danced around in dizzy circles, wagging his tail. He jumped onto the bed, stomped all over the astonished man, and licked his face.

The servants heard the master's cries and rushed to his aid. They picked up sticks and chased the donkey out of the house, giving him a good beating to teach him a lesson. The donkey never again tried to seek the master's attention, preferring to remain in the farmyard.

THE DOG AND THE WOLF

 wolf was out hunting when he came across a large, well-groomed dog, engaged in the same occupation. They fell into conversation. The wolf asked what sort of life the dog led. The dog told him how well fed and comfortable he was, living with his master. The wolf envied this life of luxury and asked what tasks the dog had to perform in exchange for the master's kindness toward him. The dog told of how he guarded the house and allowed himself to be petted by the children. The wolf thought it sounded an ideal life. Then he noticed a mark around the dog's neck and asked how he came by it. The dog explained that it was where his collar, to which his chain was attached, rubbed away at his fur. "Good-bye!" called the wolf, as he ran off.

"Wait!" said the dog, disappointed at losing his new friend. "I thought you might like to come home with me."

"No thank you," said the wolf with a laugh. "I prefer my freedom."

HOW THE HORSE BECAME MAN'S SERVANT

horse was angry at the way a wild boar insisted on entering his field and behaving as though the field was his own. He asked the boar to leave and not return, but his polite requests were ignored. The horse resorted to asking a hunter for help in ridding him of the nuisance. The man was happy to help, but only if the horse would wear a bridle and allow himself to be ridden and used in return. The horse was so incensed by the boar's behavior that he agreed, and so it was that he became man's servant.

THE BALD KNIGHT

n elderly knight was riding with some friends when a sudden gust of wind blew off his wig, revealing him to be completely bald! His friends laughed merrily, and he too joined in the laughter, saying, "It is not surprising that my wig would not stay put, when my own hair refused to do so."

THE ASTRONOMER

A man was fascinated by astronomy and spent all his time gazing into the night sky. On one occasion, a large oak was obscuring his vision, and as he wandered through the darkness to get a better view, he fell down a well. Shocked and bruised, he cried out for help, and was heard by a neighbor. She peered into the well and said, "It is hard to imagine what you see of the stars, when you do not see what is directly under your feet!"

THE MISER AND THE STONE

 miser sold all that he owned for a large piece of gold. Afraid that the gold might be lost or stolen, he dug a hole in the ground and buried it. Each day he dug it up to ensure that it was still there, for it meant all the world to him. However, he was being watched and one day the hole was empty. The miser howled with grief, tore out his hair, and acted like a madman. A neighbor who heard his bad news gave him this advice: "Take a stone, bury it, and imagine it to be gold, for lying in the ground it will serve exactly the same purpose!"

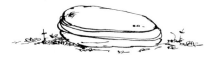

THE VAIN JACKDAW

 jackdaw so much admired the grace and beauty of peacocks, he wished to be one. He adorned himself with peacock feathers gathered from the ground. Then, shunning the company of his fellow jackdaws, he walked among the peacocks. The peacocks thought his pretense ridiculous, and laughed at him and plucked off the colorful feathers. He was so humiliated that he reluctantly went back to his own kind. But the jackdaws did not forget that he had turned against them and so they, too, rejected him and sent him on his way.

THE MILKMAID AND THE PAIL

While going about her duties as a milkmaid, a young girl mused, "With the money from the sale of this milk I could buy three hundred eggs. Allowing for some failures, I'd have at least two hundred and fifty chicks. Then by the new year they could be sold for the highest price. With all that money I could buy myself a beautiful dress and wear it to the village dance, and the young farmers would ask for my hand. But I would just smile and toss my head. . . ." With that the milkmaid did indeed toss her head, and the milk pail overbalanced. That was the end of the milk and of her fantasies.

THE HEN AND THE FOX

A fox spied a hen perched high in the rafters of a barn and tried to coax her down. "I am worried about you today, sister," he said. "You are not looking as well as you should. Come down and I will take your pulse and see if there is anything I can do for you."

The hen replied, "Yes, I do feel ill, so much so that I am afraid I will catch my death if I come down."

THE CROW AND THE PITCHER

During a long hot summer, a thirsty crow was on the lookout for water when he saw a pitcher. He peered inside and was over-joyed to see some water at the bottom. He dipped his beak in as far as he possibly could, but he could not reach the water. He tried to knock the pitcher over, but it was too heavy to move. He refused to give up. One by one, he collected pebbles and dropped them into the pitcher until he raised the water level high enough to reach with his beak, thus satisfying his thirst.

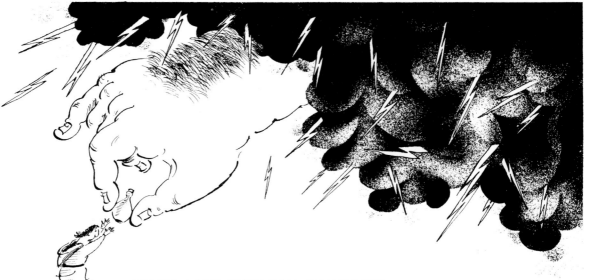

ZEUS AND THE JAR OF HOPE

Zeus collected all the good things of life together and put them in a jar to keep. He entrusted the jar to a man to look after but did not tell him what was in it. Soon the man became overwhelmed with curiosity and opened the stopper to peep inside. The good things of life escaped from the jar and flew up to heaven. The man fixed the stopper back into the jar as quickly as he could, but all he managed to save was Hope.

THE TWO POTS

Two pots, one of brass and one of earthenware, were placed on a riverbank. When the waters rose, they were caught up and swept downstream. The brass pot called to the earthenware pot, "Stay close or we will lose sight of each other."

The earthenware pot replied, "I am afraid that we must part, for if the force of the current should wash us together, I should surely be the one to suffer."

THE GOOSE THAT LAID THE GOLDEN EGGS

 man was lucky enough to own a goose that laid golden eggs, but he became impatient and greedy and was unwilling to wait for her to lay. So he killed his goose, expecting to find her full of gold, but inside she was just like any other goose, and that was the end of his good fortune.

THE MICE AND THE WEASELS AT WAR

ar was raging between the mice and the weasels. The weasels were winning and the mice were very worried. They reasoned that their failures were due to a lack of leadership and to remedy this they appointed their best fighters as generals. So that they could be readily identified, the generals were issued helmets. The next battle fought between the two enemies went the same way, however, and soon the mice were in retreat. They reached the safety of home and scuttled into their holes, all except the generals. Their large helmets stuck fast in the holes, and they were caught by the weasels.

THE FOX AND THE FIRE

farmer was beside himself with rage when he found that his henhouse had been raided by a fox. He caught the culprit and punished him by setting fire to his tail. The fox made his escape by running through the farmer's cornfields, but as he ran, his tail set the ripe corn ablaze and destroyed it.

THE LION AND THE ASS

A lion asked an ass to join him on a hunting trip. They arrived at a cave where they knew a family of goats to be. The plan was for the ass to enter the cave and kick up a terrible fuss that would frighten the goats out into the open, where they would be at the mercy of the lion. The plan worked very well, and the lion was pleased with himself. The ass, hoping for a little praise, asked the lion if he had brayed loudly enough. The lion answered, "You played your part well. You would have frightened me, too, if I hadn't known you were an ass."

THE HORSE AND THE ASS

A horse and an ass had the same master. When they traveled together, the horse was given very little to carry, apart from a saddle and a small pack, while the ass was always heavily laden. When he became old and frail, the ass found the work a great trial. One day he had so little strength left that he asked the horse for help. The horse had no sympathy for him and refused to share the heavy load. They went on their way in silence until the ass collapsed and died in the roadway. The master unburdened the ass at last and packed the load onto the horse's back, which buckled under the weight. The horse groaned and said, "Alas, if I had shared part of the ass's load, I would not have brought this hardship upon myself."

THE ASS AND THE RELIC

When an ass and his master were on a journey, the ass noticed that people made way for him and bowed down as he passed. Feeling thrilled and elated by this special treatment, the ass stopped and refused to move on until his master showed him the same kind of respect. His master, however, took a stick to him, saying, "You must be a stupid creature indeed, to imagine that men are paying homage to you, and not to the religious statue on your back."

THE ASS AND THE SALT

An ass was making a journey heavily laden with bags of salt. As he walked along a path next to the river, he slipped on the mud and plunged into the water. He pulled himself out and went on his way. His bags felt curiously light, and for a moment he thought he had lost them, but when he looked around, he saw that they were still in place, and empty. He realized that the salt must have dissolved in the water.

Some days later, on another trip by the river, he deliberately fell in, hoping that the water would once again lighten his load. This time, however, the bags were packed with sponges. Once filled with water, they were so heavy that he could hardly drag himself back onto the riverbank, and he almost drowned.

INDUSTRY AND SLOTH

An idle man was asked why he lay abed so long each day. He replied, "I have two daughters. One I call Industry, the other Sloth. Each morning they come into my bedroom, and one orders me up, but the other tells me to lie still. In fairness, I give both sides a good hearing, and by the time they have finished, the day is half over."

THE LION AND THE MOUSE

A lion was idling in the sun, pretending to sleep, when he felt a tickle on his nose. He opened one eye and, with a swipe of his huge paw, caught a small mouse trying to run away. The lion roared angrily and tossed the mouse into the air. The mouse cried, "Please don't hurt me! If only you will spare my life, I promise I will repay you." Surprised and amused by the little creature's earnest promise, the lion laughed and let the mouse go.

Time passed, and then one day the lion became ensnared in a trap. As he struggled to free himself, the ropes tightened around him until he couldn't move. The little mouse was close by and heard the lion's roars. She came and set the lion free by gnawing through the ropes. "When you kindly spared my life," said the mouse, "you laughed at the idea that one day I would repay you."

THE DOVE AND THE BEE

dove noticed that a bee had been caught up in the swirling waters of the river and was being helplessly washed downstream. Saddened by the bee's plight and determined to help, the bird snapped a branch off a nearby tree and dropped it into the water. The bee climbed up onto the branch and, once she had recovered her strength, flew away. A while later, the dove was in danger of being netted by a fowler. Just as the trap was about to fall, the bee repaid the dove by giving the man a sharp sting, causing him to miss the bird, who flew away to safety.

A BEAR WITH A SORE HEAD

A bear came across a beehive and sniffed around it with some interest. A bee, making her way back to the hive, was dismayed to see the bear, sure he was up to no good. As a warning, the bee stung the bear on the nose, then disappeared into the hive. Instead of being warned, the enraged bear struck out at the hive with his huge paw and knocked it over, disturbing the nest. The bees swarmed out of the hive and around the bear's head, inflicting hundreds of tiny stings upon him. His only means of escape was the nearby river, so the bear jumped into the water and saved himself.

THE EAGLE AND THE FARMHAND

A farmhand found an eagle ensnared in a trap. Taking great care not to damage the bird's wings, he set him free and watched with admiration as he soared into the air. Later, the man was sitting against an old stone wall, taking a rest. The bird swooped down and with his talons caught up the man's hat and dropped it some distance away. The farmhand jumped up and ran to fetch the hat, but before he could return to his resting place, the wall he had been leaning against toppled and smashed to the ground. Raising his hat to the eagle, the man thanked him for saving his life.

THE DANCING CAMEL

The animals held a meeting and, when all the formalities were over, a monkey jumped up and danced a jig. Everyone was delighted and clapped and cheered for more. A camel was watching and wished that he, too, could be popular and admired by the crowd. His longing overcame him, and he suddenly pushed the monkey out of the way and proceeded to perform a dance of his own. But the cheerful mood of the audience turned to whistles and jeers, and finally the poor camel could bear the humiliation no longer and ran away.

THE LION AND THE HARE

 hare had fallen prey to a lion and was about to be killed when a deer ran by. Tempted by a much bigger prize, the lion released the hare and chased after the deer. He had spent most of his energy in pursuit of the hare, so he soon tired, and the deer got away. "Nothing's lost," the lion said with a shrug. "I'll just go back for the hare." But when he returned, the hare had run away. The tired and hungry lion stamped his paw angrily and said, "I have only myself to blame. I should have been satisfied with what I had, and not gone after something better."

THE FOX AND THE MASK

A fox found an actor's mask and admired it, for it was the work of a talented artisan. He held it up in his paws and said, "What a pity such a splendid head should be empty of brains."

THE LION CUB

A lioness listened as a group of animals boasted of their large families. Knowing that the lioness had only one cub, a vixen asked smugly, "And how large is your family?"

The lioness calmly replied, "I have just one child, but that one is a lion."

THE POLITICAL HARE

A hare liked to stand up in public and express his belief that everyone should have fair shares in everything. A lion walked up to the speaker and, towering over him menacingly, said, "Nice words, friend, but they lack tooth and claw, such as I have."

THE CRAB AND HER BABY

 mother crab was cross with her off-spring. She said, "Why don't you walk in a straightforward fashion, instead of wandering about sideways?"

The youngster answered, "You show me how, Mother, and I will imitate you."

THE THORN IN THE LION'S PAW

 thorn had stuck fast into a lion's paw, causing him a good deal of pain and dis-comfort. A man noticed his distress and bravely went to his aid. Speaking sooth-ingly to the animal, the man approached him, lifted his paw into his lap, and removed the offending thorn. The lion was able to go on his way with scarcely a limp. Sometime later, the man was wrongfully accused of a crime and was sentenced to be flung into the lion's den. He was taken to the arena, watched by a screaming mob, and set before the hungry lion. However, just as the lion was about to maul him, the animal recognized the man as the kindly stranger who had tended to his paw. The crowd was silenced as the vicious animal tenderly placed his paw in the man's lap and rubbed his great head affectionately against him. By popular demand the man was given a pardon, and both he and the lion were set free.

THE LION IN LOVE

ong ago, a lion fell madly in love with a beautiful young girl and asked her father for her hand in marriage. The lion was determined to have his own way, and when the father hesitated, he became very fierce. Thinking quickly, the girl's father said, "Of course, I would welcome you as my son-in-law, but your long claws and sharp teeth frighten my daughter. If you were to have them removed, I am sure she would consent to be your bride." So the lion sacrificed his claws and teeth and returned to claim his bride. The girl's father inspected his soft paws and smooth gums and, once he was sure that the lion was harmless, chased him deep into the forest with a big stick.

THE MOUSE IN THE CHEST

A mouse had lived her entire life in a chest, feeding off the contents, and was quite happy to live there forevermore. One day the lid was left open, and the mouse was amusing herself by balancing on the rim when she fell over the side. The poor little mouse panicked and tried desperately to scramble up the side of the chest, but fell down again. Trying to find another way back in, she found a tasty tidbit of food, and said in amazement, "How simple I have been, to have imagined that the only good things in life were inside that chest!"

THE FOX AND THE GOAT

A fox had fallen into a well. Although it was not deep, he was unable to climb out. A goat passed by and, being thirsty, asked the fox if there was water in the well. Seeing a chance of escape, the fox replied, "The water down here is the sweetest I have ever tasted, and there is plenty for two. Why don't you join me and we will share it?" Without another thought, the goat jumped in. At once the fox jumped onto the goat's back, onto the tips of his horns, then out of the well, leaving the poor goat trapped below. As he ran off, he called over his shoulder, "You foolish goat! If only you had thought of a way out before you jumped in."

THE EAGLE, THE OWL, AND THEIR YOUNG

 he eagle and the owl were fast friends and resolved never to harm each other or any member of each other's family. "How shall I recognize your babies?" the eagle asked the owl.

"That's easy," answered the owl proudly, "for mine are always bigger and more beautiful than other youngsters."

Sometime later, the eagle came across a nest of scraggly young chicks and wondered to whom they belonged. They were extraordinarily ugly, with tangled feathers and big staring eyes. "At least," he thought, "I can be sure that they do not belong to my friend the owl!" With that he partook of lunch until the nest was empty. Just as he was about to leave, the owl returned to her nest. "Where are my babies?" she cried.

"They are gone," answered the eagle, "and you are to blame, for painting such an unlikely picture of them."

THE HORSE AND THE WOLF

fter a long, harsh winter, a wolf was out hunting for food. "A hen, or better still a plump sheep, would be ideal," he thought, for he was very hungry. These delicacies were not to be found, but instead he saw a horse grazing in a field. The wolf knew that catching him would take much cunning, so he acted the part of a physician in order to draw close to the horse and win its trust. The horse was not fooled by this chicanery, however. He asked the "physician" if he would be good enough to look at one of his hooves, which had been troubling him. The wolf was only too pleased to oblige, and bent down in a professional manner to inspect the hoof. With this, the horse gave an almighty kick to the wolf's head, which sent him on his way with his ears ringing.

THE DOVE

dove looked at a painting and thought the scene was real. In it she could see a jug of water. She was thirsty, so she flew straight at the picture, hit it hard, and fell to the ground, damaging her wings.

THE FOX, THE WOLF, AND THE MOON CHEESE

fox saw the reflection of the moon in the water at the bottom of a well, and took it to be a large, round, yellow cheese. It looked so tempting that he jumped into a bucket and lowered himself down to fetch it. Once down, however, he found that he was trapped, and the cheese was not what it had seemed. Two days later a wolf came by, and the fox called up to him, "How would you like this delicious cheese? Just let yourself down in that bucket to fetch it, and it is yours."

Greed and hunger made the wolf gullible. As his bucket fell to the bottom with a bump, the fox's bucket shot to the top of the well, and out he hopped, free at last.

THE FROGS WHO WISHED FOR A KING

A group of frogs, living a quiet and tranquil life around a pond, became discontented with their lot. They wished they had a powerful leader who would make their lives more exciting. All at once, from out of the sky came a large log of wood, which plunged into the pond with a big splash. "Zeus has sent us a king!" they cried joyfully. For days they paid court to the log as it drifted majestically around the pond. But it made a poor king, and they soon tired of it, using it as a convenient resting place when crossing the water. "The king is so dull!" they complained to Zeus. This angered the god and he sent a crane to rule over them. The crane proved to be a tyrannical leader, and the frogs feared for their lives. They begged Zeus to take the crane away, and he said to them, "All right, but learn your lesson well: be content in the future."

THE MOUSE AND HIS BRIDE

A young and ambitious mouse wished to marry into a great family, and so he courted a lioness and asked her to wed him. On their wedding day, the eager mouse ran to meet his bride, but she, being giddy with excitement, unknowingly stepped on him with one of her great paws. The marriage ceremony, unfortunately, had to be canceled.

THE AGES OF MAN

A horse, an ox, and a dog felt indebted to man for his protection and kindness and wished to repay him. They resolved that each would give him a part of his own character to carry through life. The early years were chosen by the horse, bestowing upon man the tendency to be headstrong, opinionated, and impetuous in youth. The middle years were chosen by the ox, thus the middle-aged man is diligent, hardworking, and thrifty. The dog chose old age, giving the old man his selfishness and short temper.

THE BOY AND THE FILBERTS

small boy thrust his hand into a jar of filberts and grasped a fistful, but found he could not withdraw his hand without first letting go of the nuts. He burst into tears of frustration but would not let them go. The boy was given this friendly advice: "If you will be satisfied with half that amount of filberts, you will then have the use of your hand as well."

THE WOLF AND THE CRANE

wolf was eating dinner when a chicken bone became stuck in his throat, causing him great pain. A crane happened by, and the wolf promised her a reward if she would help him. The crane agreed. She looked into the wolf's gaping jaws, spied the bone, and carefully removed it with her long beak. The good deed was scarcely done when the wolf bared his teeth and said, "What are you waiting for? You had your reward when your head was in my mouth and I spared your life. Be off with you!"

CAT INTO WOMAN

A cat was so devoted to her young master she asked Aphrodite to change her into a woman so that they could marry. Her wish was granted, and the cat was transformed into a lovely young woman. The youth lost no time in asking for her hand in marriage. They lived happily together until one day the goddess tested the young woman by setting a mouse down before her. With lightning reflexes the woman chased it, caught it up, and got ready to devour it. The goddess knew then that the woman was still a cat at heart and changed her back to her former self.

THE ANT AND THE GRASSHOPPER

One winter's morning an ant was checking his larder to ensure that the grain, carefully harvested and stored in previous years, was in good condition. A cold and bedraggled grasshopper passed by and, seeing the grain, stopped to beg a little for himself. "I collected my grain last year," said the ant. "Why didn't you?" The grasshopper explained that he had been too busy dancing and singing to plan ahead. The ant was irritated by his attitude and said sharply, "In that case, you had better dance and sing your way through the winter, too."

THE ASS IN A LION'S SKIN

When an ass found a lion's skin, it amused him to put it on his back and roam the countryside, spreading alarm among the animals. He saw a fox and, knowing the crafty fellow would be hard to trick, jumped out at him with a great roar. But the fox merely sighed in a bored manner and said, "I cannot be afraid of a lion who brays like an ass!"

THE STAG'S REFLECTION

A stag was drinking at a pool and, seeing his own reflection, paused to admire his antlers. As he gazed at himself, however, he became critical of his legs and hooves, wishing they looked as magnificent as his antlers. His thoughts were interrupted by hunters, and he turned tail and sped off toward cover. His long powerful legs took him deep into the forest, leaving the hunters behind, but his antlers became entangled in low-hanging branches. As he struggled to free himself, he said, "My legs, which I reviled, are my strength, but my antlers, which I took pride in, could be my downfall."

THE OX AND THE HEIFER

heifer was idly watching the efforts of a hardworking ox who was laboring in the field. Each time he passed by, the cheeky heifer tormented him with gibes. "What an old drudge you are!" she called rudely. Later in the day, when work was done, the ox was led off to a clean stall and rewarded for his toil with good food and fresh water. More than content with his lot, he saw the heifer being led away for sacrifice and thought, "I would rather feel the weight of the yoke on my neck than the blade of the axe."

THE WOLF IN SHEEP'S CLOTHING

n order to make easy work of hunting for his supper, a clever wolf struck upon the idea of dressing himself as a sheep. When hungry, he put on a sheepskin and mingled with the flock. So good was the disguise that the shepherd did not notice anything amiss, and the wolf could choose his prey at his pleasure. One evening, however, the shepherd desired mutton stew for his supper, chose a suitable sheep from the flock, and slaughtered the animal—only to discover that his intended dinner was a wolf in sheep's clothing.

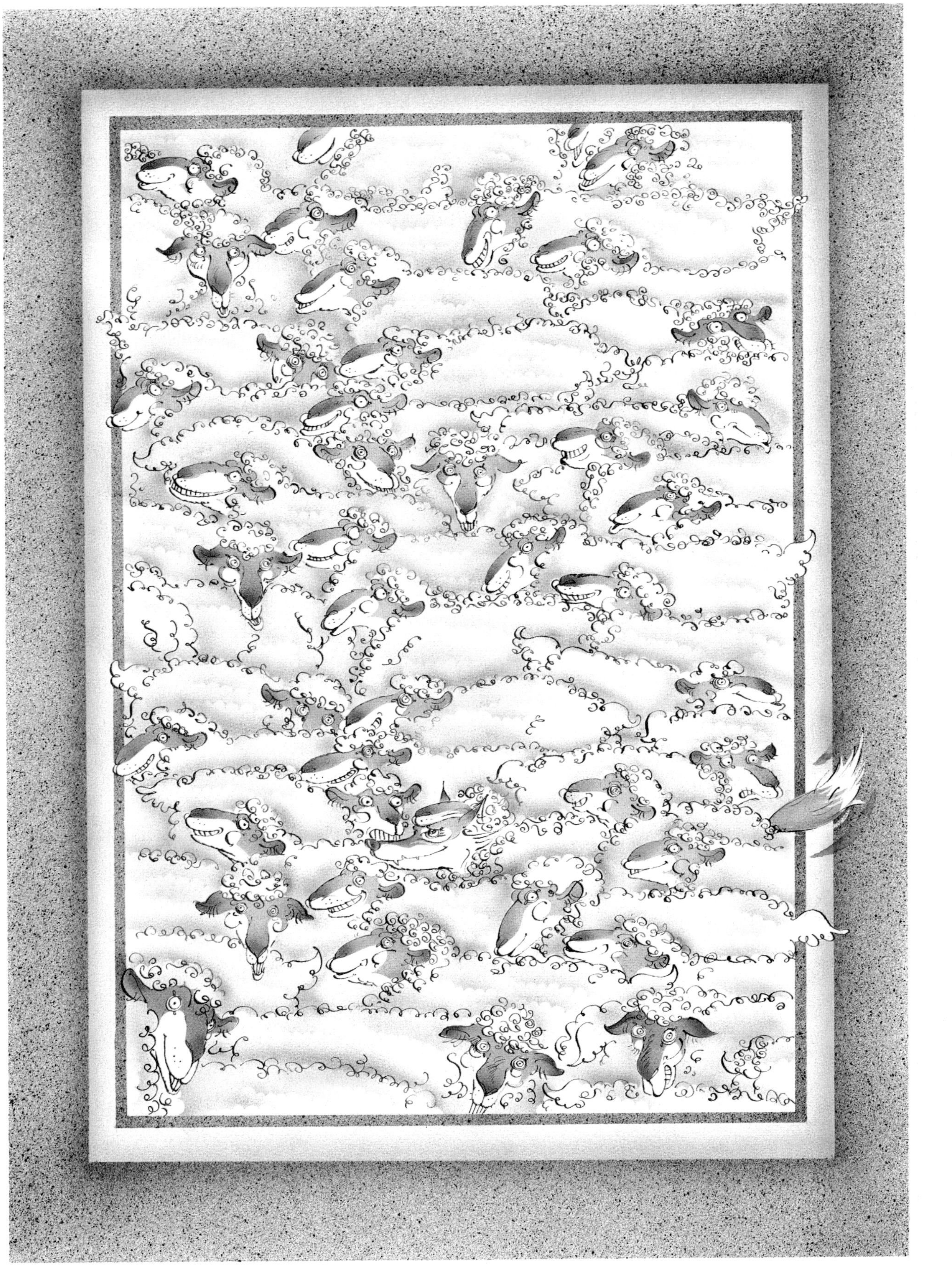

THE BUNDLE OF STICKS AT SEA

Some travelers interrupted their journey to look out to sea at what they took to be a great ship. As it sailed slowly inland, the travelers agreed that it was, in fact, not a ship but a boat. They watched as it gradually drifted onto the beach and saw that they had been wrong again. Disappointed, they complained to one another, "We have wasted all this time watching a bundle of sticks."

THE MICE IN COUNCIL

A meeting was held among the mice to discuss how they should deal with a cat who was causing them trouble. A young mouse got up and said brightly, "The way to deal with the nuisance is to tie a bell around the cat's neck. That way we will all hear him coming." The mice nodded in agreement and cheered and applauded the speaker. The meeting was about to be adjourned when a question was raised. "Just a small point," said a mouse from the back of the assembly, "but who is being given the task of tying on the bell, and how will he do it?"

THE CAT IN DISGUISE

A cat made it her duty to rid a house of mice. She was so good at her job that the mice who survived were too frightened to come out from under the floorboards, thus ending her hunting. The cat became hungry and thought of a plan for bringing the mice out into the open again. She wrapped herself in some old sacking and draped herself over a hook on the wall, pretending to be a shopping bag. She kept very still for a long time, as only a cat can, and waited for the mice.

Eventually the mice were brave enough to look out, and they saw the bag hanging on the wall. "That bag wasn't there before," said one of them.

"Don't go near it," warned another. "I've never seen a shopping bag with a tail before!"

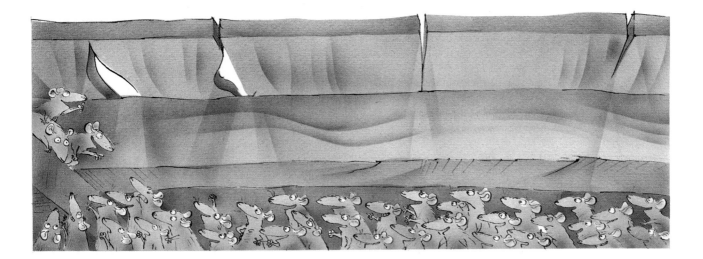

THE LION'S COURT

A lion issued a decree to all his subjects, demanding that they should each come to court to be presented. When they arrived they were summoned to his chamber, an unpleasant room that had a most obnoxious odor. A bear was first to enter, but he stopped in his tracks and covered his nose, unable to hide his distaste at the stench. The lion was dreadfully insulted and had the bear taken away and imprisoned. A monkey, next in line, was determined not to make the same mistake as the bear. He said, "O sumptuous chamber! And filled with sweet fragrance! Is the scent rose or lavender? Or some exotic mixture of . . ."

The lion stopped this transparent flattery and sent the monkey off to join the bear. "What do you have to say on this subject?" he asked the fox, who was the next to be presented.

"I am unable to comment, Your Majesty, for I have a head cold and cannot smell a thing," the fox replied cleverly, and was allowed to go on his way.

TITLE INDEX